10/93

COLLEGE TERRACE BRANCH

Palo Alto City Library

The individual borrower is responsible for all library material borrowed on his or her card.

Charges as determined by the CITY OF PALO ALTO will be assessed for each overdue item.

Damaged or non-returned property will be billed to the individual borrower by the CITY OF PALO ALTO.

P.O. Box 10250, Palo Alto, CA 94303

GAYLORD

CAPTAIN
CAT

An I Can Read Book®

CAPTAIN CAT

Story and pictures by

SYD HOFF

HarperCollins*Publishers*

I Can Read Book is a registered trademark of HarperCollins Publishers.

Captain Cat
Copyright © 1993 by Syd Hoff
Printed in the U.S.A. All rights reserved.
1 2 3 4 5 6 7 8 9 10

First Edition

Library of Congress Cataloging-in-Publication Data
Hoff, Syd, date
  Captain Cat : story and pictures / by Syd Hoff.
    p.   cm. — (An I can read book)
  Summary: A cat makes friends with a soldier and learns about military life
when he joins the army.
  ISBN 0-06-020527-X. — ISBN 0-06-020528-8 (lib. bdg.)
  [1. Cats—Fiction.   2. United States.   Army—Fiction.]   I. Title.
II. Series.
PZ7.H672Cap   1993   91-27518
[E]—dc20   CIP
                                                                  AC

For Nina

6

Captain Cat joined the army.

He went in when nobody was looking.

7

The soldiers marched in a parade.

"Left, right—

left, right . . ."

Captain Cat kept in step.

He knew one foot from the other.

11

"That cat has more stripes
than we have,"
said a corporal to a sergeant.

"Meow," said Captain Cat.

The sergeant looked at the cat.

"Yes sir!"

said the sergeant, and laughed.

From then on

everybody started saying,

"Here, Captain Cat,"

when they wanted him,

instead of

"Here, kitty kitty."

But sometimes the soldiers

had no time for Captain Cat.

16

"I have to clean the bathrooms,"

said one soldier.

"I have to sweep the grounds,"

said another soldier.

One soldier named Pete

always found time for Captain Cat,

even when he was on guard duty.

"You remind me of a cat back home,"

he said, and scratched Captain Cat

behind the ears.

Pete played with Captain Cat so much,

20

he got into trouble.

The general made Pete

do kitchen duty.

Captain Cat kept him company.

Pete let Captain Cat play

with the potato peels.

"Are you my buddy?"

asked Pete.

"Me-ow," said Captain Cat.

The next morning

a bugle blew.

Oh, how Pete hated to get up!

But Captain Cat

sprang right out of bed.

25

He had to check out the garbage

before it was taken away.

Then it was time for inspection.

Everybody lined up.

Captain Cat lined up, too.

The general fixed a soldier's gun.

He fixed Pete's hat.

All he could fix for Captain Cat
were his whiskers.

"Forward march!" said the general.

The soldiers went one way.

Captain Cat went the other way.

He had to chase some birds.

The soldiers crawled

in the mud.

They hiked

through rain and sleet.

But not Captain Cat!
He was taking a nap
on Pete's bed.

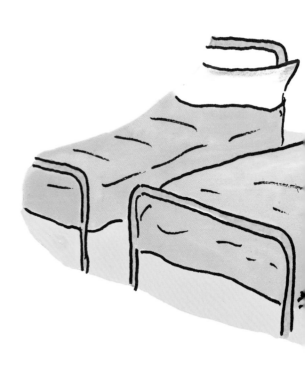

Time for chow!

Pete and the other soldiers

rushed into the mess hall

to get plates of nice, hot food.

Captain Cat wished

Pete would get him

a plate with a mouse.

"Are you my buddy?" asked Pete.

"Me-ow," said Captain Cat.

Lights out!

Everyone went to sleep

and dreamed of loved ones.

44

Captain Cat dreamed

of his loved one, too.